To Mum and Dad,
who let me follow my star A.M.

To Mum and Dad, and all
my friends who posed so patiently A.R.

Text copyright © 1999 Alan MacDonald
Illustrations copyright © 1999 Andrew Rowland
This edition copyright © 1999 Lion Publishing

The moral rights of the author and illustrator
have been asserted

Published by
Lion Publishing plc
Sandy Lane West, Oxford, England
www.lion-publishing.co.uk
ISBN 0 7459 3892 2

First edition 1999
10 9 8 7 6 5 4 3 2 1 0

A catalogue record for this book is available
from the British Library

Typeset in 19/22 Baskerville MT Schoolbook
Printed and bound in Malaysia

The Not-So-Wise Man

Alan MacDonald

Illustrations by
Andrew Rowland

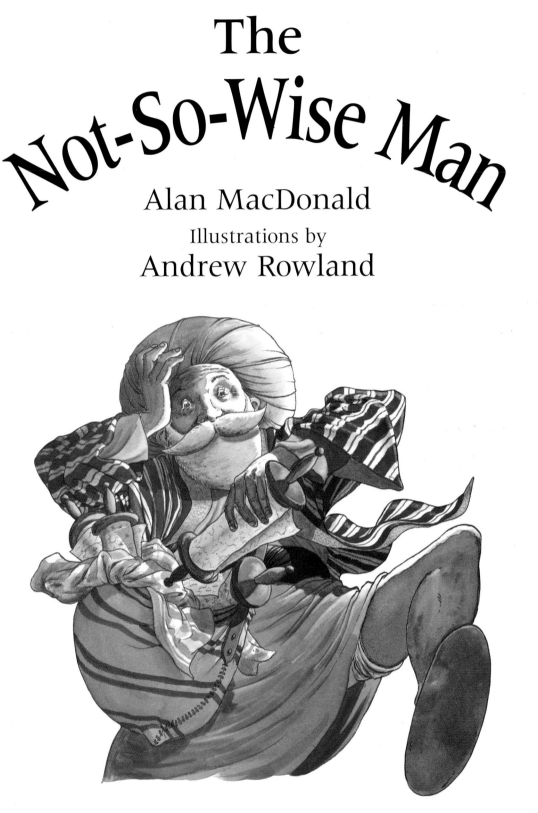

LION
Children's Books

Ashtar was wise, the wisest
in the land, so people said.
He lived alone in a tall
windswept tower
at the top of a hill.

People came from far and wide to listen to Ashtar's great learning. They crowded into Ashtar's tower, sitting on the stairs and peering through the door.

Ashtar told them about a time to come when a great king would be born. 'A wise man should be ready,' he said, 'for this child will come from heaven itself.'

When the last visitor had gone, Ashtar climbed the winding stairs to the top of his tower and gazed up into the sky, as he did every night. The stars shone like a spray of diamonds. Ashtar knew each one and counted them off in his head.

Suddenly he stopped. His old heart leapt. There in the midnight blue was the sign he'd been waiting for—a new star in the sky.

He ran downstairs. He threw his scrolls and
a clean nightshirt into his bag. A wise man
travels light.

The star was calling him to follow. The king
from heaven was about to be born and Ashtar
longed to see the child for himself.

All that night he journeyed, following the bright star. He crossed great mountains and crept by villages sleeping under the pale moon.

At last, crossing a plain, he met some travellers dressed in rich silks and furs.

'We have come a long way and our camels are tired,' they said. 'Do you know anywhere we can find water?'

Ashtar put his ear to the ground and listened. Then he stood up and sniffed the wind. 'Over that hill you'll find a pool of water where you can rest and drink,' he said.

The travellers marvelled at Ashtar's wisdom. They asked him to join them on their journey.

'We too are following a star. Why not come with us?'

But Ashtar shook his head. 'A wise man travels alone,' he said.

Eager to be on his way, Ashtar left the travellers
and set off on his quest again.

The next night, Ashtar heard voices calling at
the edge of a wood. Three shepherds came out of
the darkness, carrying torches.

'What are you looking for?' Ashtar asked them.

'One of our sheep,' said the shepherds. 'It's run away.'

Ashtar pointed to a tuft of wool caught on a bush. 'Follow the trail into the wood; that's where you'll find your sheep.'

The shepherds found the sheep just as Ashtar had said. They begged him to stop and warm himself by their fire. 'The night is cold and the road is long. Stay with us and talk a while. It's not often we meet such a clever man.'

'Thank you, but I must go on with my journey,' said Ashtar. 'A wise man has few words to spare.'

So Ashtar rode on his way, thinking it must be
the wind singing so softly over the hills.

Before long, he reached a small town where the streets were crowded with people. He knocked at the door of an inn.

The innkeeper stuck his head out, impatiently. 'No room! We're full up. How many times do I have to tell people?'

Ashtar smiled. 'A wise man would put a sign on the door. That way he could get some peace.'

The idea had never occurred to the innkeeper. He wrote 'No Room' on a sign and nailed it to the door.

The next people who came to the door didn't
knock. They saw the sign and turned away sadly,
the man leading his donkey with a pale, weary
woman on its back.

The innkeeper watched them go, delighted. He'd get some peace at last. To show Ashtar his thanks, he promised to find him a bed for the night.

Past midnight, Ashtar woke up. The star shone through his window, filling the room with silver light. Ashtar dressed hurriedly and went out.

He walked through the still, silent streets, searching. Perhaps it was in this very town that the child from heaven would be born.

At last, beside a small inn, he came to a ramshackle stable.

Ashtar could hear cows lowing inside. Grazing under a tree were a donkey and a flock of sheep. He wondered who could own so many animals.

But it was no business of his. He had come looking for a king and he wasn't foolish enough to think that a poor stable was the place.

Sighing deeply, Ashtar turned back and went on his way. The wisest man in all the land was going home, none the wiser.